Level 9

William Stobbs
Gregory's Garden

Oxford University Press

Oxford Toronto Melbourne

Gregory dug the soil.

The birds ate the worms and beetles.

Gregory planted the seeds.

The birds ate them up.

Some of the seeds grew.

Rabbits, squirrels, and a hedgehog ate them up.

Gregory guarded the pumpkin,
and the weeds grew.

The wild flowers grew.

And so did the pumpkin.

When the wild flowers died,
the pumpkin turned orange.

'It was a good year for pumpkins,'
Gregory told the Snowman.

Oxford University Press, Walton Street, Oxford OX2 6DP

Oxford New York Toronto
Delhi Bombay Calcutta Madras Karachi
Kuala Lumpur Singapore Hong Kong Tokyo
Nairobi Dar es Salaam Cape Town
Melbourne Auckland Madrid

and associated companies in
Berlin Ibadan

Oxford is a trade mark of Oxford University Press

First Published 1984
Reprinted 1985, 1986, 1987, 1990, 1991, 1993

British Library Cataloguing in Publications Data
Stobbs, William
Gregory's Garden.
I. Title
823'.914[J] PZ7
ISBN 0-19-272140-2

Typeset by Set Fair Ltd.
Printed in Hong Kong